The Haunting of Grade Three

The Haunting of Grade Three

by Grace Maccarone

illustrated by Kelly Oechsli

SCHOLASTIC INC.

New York   Toronto   London   Auckland   Sydney

Grateful acknowledgment is made to Golden Torch
Music Corp. and Raydiola Music for their
permission to reprint "I ain't 'fraid of no ghosts"
from "GHOSTBUSTERS" by Ray Parker, Jr.
© 1984 by Golden Torch Music Corp. and Raydiola Music.
Used by permission. All rights reserved.

ISBN 0-590-43868-9

24 23 22   9/9 0 1/0

Printed in the U.S.A.   **40**

To Mom and Dad

Chapter One

ADAM TURNED OFF the VCR and laughed. "I ain't 'fraid of no ghosts." He heard the words again and again in his head.

Ghostbusters was his favorite movie. Three scientists lost their jobs. So what did they do? They weren't afraid of ghosts. They bought an old fire station and started a business. A ghost-catching business!

The three scientists chased ghosts all over the city. They went after ghosts that looked like people, ghosts that looked like skeletons, ghosts that looked like monsters, and ghosts that looked like blobs.

It was just the kind of job Adam could see himself doing someday!

Adam felt a breeze. The living room curtains ballooned and swayed. Adam jumped off the couch and pretended to blast away.

"A class five vapor," he said. It was shapeless, see-through, and mean. "That's it for you, you green slob."

Adam carefully stepped over the imaginary dead ghost and walked to the kitchen. His brother, Tim, was having Ring Dings and milk with their older sister, Lisa.

Lisa had some blue stuff in her hair tonight and blue polish on her nails. Her lipstick was white, and she wore two different earrings. Her dress and stockings were black.

Lisa hadn't looked like that last year. She had looked normal then. But tonight, Adam thought, she could easily have passed as the bride of Frankenstein.

"You going to a Halloween party?" Adam teased.

"No such luck," she answered. "I'm stuck here with you guys tonight. Mom and Dad went to the movies with Ellen and Jeff Parish."

"You promised to tell me a story," Tim said. "A scary one."

Lisa thought for a minute.

"I've got a good one," she said. "And it's true. It's about Blackwell House."

Adam was curious.

"Yeah? What do you know about Blackwell House?" he asked.

There were so many kids in Elmwood Elementary that the school building couldn't hold them all. This year, the whole third grade was in a separate building — the old Blackwell mansion. Or as the third-graders called it, the old spook house.

The building had been fixed up with paint, plumbing, blackboards, desks, and chairs. But even with bright paint and posters, it was still a creepy place.

Adam loved it.

"I ain't 'fraid of no ghosts."

Chapter Two

TIM SQUIRMED IN his seat. "So let's hear the story," he said.

Lisa lit a candle, then turned off the kitchen light. As she leaned toward the candle, it cast an orange glow and eerie shadows on her face.

Adam felt a cozy creepiness as Lisa began her story:

Ten years ago, two college students took a trip across the country. They didn't have much money. They often slept in buses and trains as they traveled from town to town. Sometimes they camped out.

That night, the students planned to camp outside of Elmwood. But it started to rain. They saw an empty old house. It looked so warm and dry that the students decided to wait out the storm inside.

They didn't know it, but they were entering a haunted house. Blackwell House.

The students explored all the rooms while there was still daylight. "Hello! Hello!" they shouted. But no one answered. They set up their sleeping bags in the large parlor downstairs and fell asleep — but not for long.

Soon they were awakened by the sound of footsteps overhead. Thump, thump, thump, thump.

A door swung — back and forth, back and forth.

Then BANG! A door slammed shut. And BANG! went another and another and another.

The walls shook. BOOM! An explosion.

"Ghosts!" said one of the students.

"Aw, there's no such thing," said the other.

The students lay perfectly still. For several minutes, all was quiet. The thumping and swinging and slamming and booming had stopped. But a strange sound was coming from upstairs.

"WooOOoowooOOoowooOOoo. . . . "

"What's that?"

"Just the wind. I'll prove it," said the boy as he walked up the stairs.

And again he heard the sound.

"WooOOoowooOOoowooOOoo. . . . "

It was coming from one of the bedrooms. Slowly, he turned the knob and opened the door.

Lightning flashed. Thunder roared. From the far wall, a ghostly skull looked him in the eye!

And again he heard the sound.

"WooOOoowooOOoowooOOoo. . . . "

The student screamed, "Let's get out of here!"

He ran down the stairs and out of the house. His friend followed close behind. And no one has ever heard from them since.

"Just as I suspected," said Adam. "Blackwell House *is* haunted!"

"There's no such thing as a ghost," said Tim. Then he screamed. "Aaaaaaah!"

Two shiny eyes glowed in the dark.

But it was only the cat, Casper.

Adam and Lisa laughed. Then Lisa spoke in a slow, mysterious whisper. "Maybe. Maybe not." She blew out the candle and turned on the kitchen light.

Chapter Three

"I'VE GOT TO get to bed," Adam said.

It was late. Adam fed his turtle, Samantha, before turning out the light in his room.

The next day was a school day, and Adam had a math test. He hoped he had studied hard enough.

That night, Adam had a dream.

He had written a letter to the students in Lisa's story, but he did not know their address. He had to find the right mailbox to put it in. He searched and searched, and then he found it. He didn't know why, but he was sure it was the right one.

The mailbox was black with a skull and crossbones on it. Adam held back. Something wasn't right. But he had to mail that letter. Adam opened the door.

Out came a horrible ghost — the same color as the living room curtains. Out came another ghost and another and another. They leaped and swirled around his head. And as they danced, they chanted the multiplication tables.

"Six times seven equals forty-two; seven times seven equals forty-nine; eight times seven equals fifty-six; nine times seven equals sixty-three."

Then he heard his name. "Adam! Adam!"

"Adam, wake up! You're yelling in your sleep!" It was Tim.

Adam looked at the clock. The alarm would ring soon, anyway. He got out of bed and went into the living room. He took a shot at the curtain.

"Gotcha last," he said. Then he curled up on the couch with his math book.

"Two times eight equals sixteen; three times eight equals twenty-four; four times eight equals thirty-two. . . ."

Chapter Four

BLACKWELL HOUSE WAS half a mile away from its nearest neighbor. Adam had just reached the long road that led to the building.

In front of him were other third-graders. Most walked in small groups of two or three, though there was also one big mob of eight — and a few loners who were waiting on the front steps for their friends.

The road was lined by tall trees and dense bushes. Adam loved to think of all sorts of creepy, crawly things that might live there.

"Hey, Adam, wait up!"

It was Chuck Webber, looking as if he'd gotten dressed in front of an electric fan. His gray sweat shirt was inside out. Its sleeves were cut off at the elbow. The hem of his jeans dragged along the ground because he'd forgotten to put on a belt.

"Ready for another day at the old spook house?" Chuck asked.

"Hey, I heard a story about Blackwell House that you won't believe," said Adam.

Just then, little Joey Baker ran up to them. As usual, he was dressed in clothes that were two years out of style.

"Hey, guys," he said in his high squeaky voice, "you'll never guess what I saw in the boys' room yesterday! A real live ghost!"

Chuck laughed. "I'll bet you did. You also said that your father worked for the FBI and your mother was a scientist and you were born in a jungle. That was after you said your father was a four-star general, your mother was an astronaut, and you were born in China."

"Well, this is the truth!" said Joey. "You guys will be sorry."

Then he ran off to look for someone who would believe him.

"What a funny kid," said Adam. "I wonder why he tells so many lies."

"Speaking of funny," said Chuck, "I've got a joke for you."

"Maybe he's telling the truth this time," said Adam.

"Will you forget about that nerd already? Listen to this."

This month, everyone was telling monster jokes. Last month, it was elephant jokes.

"What do you call a twenty-foot monster?" Chuck asked.

Adam thought about it for a while. Dracula? No, he isn't that big. Frankenstein? Probably not. "I give up," he said finally.

Chuck smiled, took off his baseball cap, and bowed. "Sir," he answered.

"That's dumb," said Adam, but he was smiling. "Now I've got one for you: What does Dracula take for a sore throat?"

"Coffin drops!" Chuck shouted. "I told you that one last week!"

Both boys were laughing as they walked toward Blackwell House. And there it was. One big monster of a building. It had dark towers, pointy gables, and shadowy arches.

"Ever notice how some houses have faces?" Adam asked.

"Huh, what do you mean?" asked Chuck.

"You know, windows for eyes and a door for the mouth."

"If you say so," said Chuck. "Then, that

one's having some Hamburger now. Gulp! I wonder if it can swallow her glasses."

Norma Hamburger was very smart and sensitive. There were some kids Chuck especially liked to tease. Among them, Norma was his favorite target.

"There goes Danny Biddicker," said Adam. "It should be pretty full after it swallows him."

Danny Biddicker was the biggest kid in the whole third grade. In fact, he was even bigger than the fourth-graders.

"I hate to break the news to you, kid," said Chuck, "but we are about to be dessert."

Adam faked a karate kick. "I won't go without a fight," he said.

"I can't bear to look," said Chuck. He covered his eyes with his hands. And he bumped right into Mrs. Pick, the reading teacher.

"Let's behave, boys," she said. "You are in school now."

The boys went up the fancy wide staircase. They passed the second floor. All the other

third grade classes were there. Then they went up a tiny staircase to the third floor.

On the way to his seat, Chuck whispered in Norma's ear. "Hold the pickles; hold the lettuce." Norma pretended not to hear.

The boys took their seats in what had once been a large bedroom. Adam grinned. There was something neat about having a fireplace in the classroom — even if it was closed up.

Adam sat next to a window — a window with many tiny pieces of glass. The glass formed pretty patterns and threw rainbow colors on the floors, desk tops, and walls. All during the day, the patterns would move and change.

Chuck poked Adam in the back and whispered, "Weren't you going to tell me something about Blackwell House?"

Adam felt Mr. Jenkins's eyes right on him. He couldn't say a word.

Chapter Five

"CLEAR YOUR DESKS for the math test," Mr. Jenkins announced.

Soon, only pencils remained on the desks of the twenty-six third-graders. Mr. Jenkins went from row to row, handing out unlined math paper.

The class folded their papers into sixteen boxes as Mr. Jenkins wrote the math problems on the blackboard. Then something strange happened.

It started with Lori Marino, who had the

first desk in the first row. One by one, Lori's three pencils slid off her desk.

The same thing happened to the pencils on Paul Lucas's desk — and on Jenny Carle's desk. Soon, all the pencils had fallen off all the desks in the first row. Mr. Jenkins turned around.

"Okay, everybody. Please settle down now," he said. Then he turned back to the board.

But the pencils kept rolling off desks — in the second row, the third row, the fourth row, and the fifth row. Mr. Jenkins turned around again. He did not look pleased.

"All right," he said. "What's going on?"

As usual, Chuck called out without raising his hand. "All the pencils are falling off our desks!"

"What?" said Mr. Jenkins. "Norma, will you tell me what happened?"

Mr. Jenkins knew he could count on Norma to tell him the truth. Norma hated it. She didn't like being the class goody-goody. But she didn't know how to act any other way.

"It's true," Norma said. "The pencils just rolled off our desks. All by themselves."

"Maybe it was a supernatural force," said Adam.

"Highly unlikely," said Mr. Jenkins.

"There's got to be a reasonable explanation," said Debbie Clark. Debbie was the class science nut. She tried to find a reasonable explanation for everything.

All of a sudden, the globe that had been sitting on a shelf near the window fell on the floor.

Then the door rattled and slammed shut.

"It's the ghosts!" Jenny Carle shouted.

"They're coming to get us! They're coming to get the whole third grade!"

Chuck laughed out loud. "Not the whole third grade," he said. "The only one they want is you!"

Some of the other kids laughed, too, until the lights began to flicker.

"Now calm down," said Mr. Jenkins. "It's just an old building; there's nothing to get excited about."

"*Old and haunted*," Chuck said in his most ghostlike voice.

"We'll take a break for recess." Mr. Jenkins sounded tired. "Line up, everyone."

Chapter Six

ONCE OUTSIDE, THE class split into two groups. The jump ropers played along the wide asphalt path. The softball players used the big flat grassy lawn.

The softball game was a close one. The score was fourteen to twelve in the bottom of the final inning.

Adam was in center field. He wasn't big or strong. But he was fast. He loved to run down those long fly balls.

Adam held up two fingers to Chuck in left field to signal that there were two outs.

They needed just one more to win the game. But Paul Lucas was on first, Debbie Clark on second. And Danny Biddicker was coming to bat. Danny could really hit.

Adam decided to play a little deeper.

CRACK!

Danny lined one right between Chuck and Adam. There was no way to catch this one. No way to knock it down, either. It was the best hit of the day.

The ball bounced all the way to the end of the playground and disappeared in the bushes. A home run!

Adam's team lost the game in the final inning. Now where were they going to find the ball?

"I'll go this way. You go that way," Chuck shouted.

Adam searched among the vines and sticker bushes without any luck. Thorny branches pricked his fingers.

He began to think about horrible creatures that might be lurking just inches away from his feet. Snakes. Rats. Lizards. Tarantulas. Or worse.

All of a sudden, Adam felt something tug at his ankle. Down he went. "Ouch!"

Adam landed on something hard and smooth. It was covered with leaves and pine needles. Adam brushed them off and found a flat stone with some writing on it:

IN MEMORY OF
THOMAS JACKSON
BLACKWELL
1853 - 1863

And there was the ball.

Adam heard footsteps.

"Are you all right?" Chuck called.

"I just got caught in some vines," Adam said, "but I'm all right. And I found the ball."

Chuck noticed the stone, too. "He was just a kid," Chuck said. Then he looked at Adam. "We'd better get going. I can hear Jenkins calling us back to the old spook house."

Chapter Seven

ADAM RAISED A dirty right hand.

"Let me guess," said Mr. Jenkins. "The boys' room. Right?"

When Adam walked into the boys' room, he noticed that one of the stall doors was closed. As he scrubbed his hands, he heard a flush.

The stall door swung open — but no one was there! Adam froze. He tried to figure out what had just happened.

Was Joey Baker telling the truth for once? Was it a ghost? Was it something else?

The big wooden door flew open. It was Danny.

"You okay, guy? You look as if you've just seen a ghost."

Adam laughed. "I ain't 'fraid of no ghosts."

But secretly, he was beginning to wonder.

As Adam and Danny walked back to their seats, Mr. Jenkins announced there would be committee work. The class had never done this before. But then, Mr. Jenkins had them do a lot of things they had never done before.

Mr. Jenkins was new to Elmwood Elementary. And so far, his students felt pretty lucky to have him.

Mr. Jenkins chose five kids to be the committee chairmen: Paul Lucas, Lori Marino, Jimmy Belsky, Kim Larson, and of course, Norma Hamburger. As committee chairmen, they had to start picking other kids for their groups.

Norma's best friend, Kim, was the head of her own committee. And Kim had already picked their other best friend, Liz. Kim and

Liz were getting friendlier lately. Today, they even wore the same purple sweater.

It was hard to have two best friends. Sometimes it was like having no best friend at all. So Norma picked Debbie Clark, a nice girl and a good student — even if she did talk a lot.

When Debbie Clark picked Adam, Chuck poked him on the shoulder. "She likes you," Chuck whispered.

Adam was embarrassed. He gave Chuck an angry look. But when his turn came, Adam picked Chuck anyway.

"Oh, good," said Chuck, just loudly enough for Norma to hear him. "I get to be on the Burger Queen's committee."

Norma shook her head. She could already see that this committee work was going to be a major pain.

During the next round, Chuck picked Danny. Chuck figured it would be good to have The Big Guy on their committee. Who knows, our committee work just might have something to do with sports, Chuck thought.

Danny didn't have a choice. Joey Baker was the last one left. So he joined their committee, too.

After the committees were picked, Mr. Jenkins gave out the assignments.

Paul's group was to be the transportation committee. They would study the river that ran on the border of Elmwood and find out how it helped the town. Everyone on the committee got excited when Mr. Jenkins said they would get to ride a ferry across the river.

Lori's group became the industry committee. They would get to go to the printing plant, where they would see how a book was made.

Jimmy's group, the communication committee, would study and visit the *Elmwood Independent* — and get a chance to write a newspaper story.

Kim Larson's group was the luckiest of all. They were the recreation committee. That meant they would study what people in Elmwood did for fun and even get to talk to some players on the Elmwood Eagles, a real double-A baseball team!

What could be left? the last group wondered. They hoped it would be as good as the others.

Mr. Jenkins smiled. "Norma, Adam, Chuck, Debbie, Joey, Dan, you will be our psychic investigation committee. You will try to figure out what's been happening here at Blackwell House. You will be our ghost hunters."

"All right!" said Adam.

The five others on the committee looked at him as if he were a martian — or even a ghost himself.

"Lucky us," said Chuck. "The other committees get to ride a ferry, write a newspaper story, watch a printing press, talk to baseball players. We get to hang out at school."

"I don't want to do this," Joey whined. "And no one can make me."

Norma chewed her fingernail as she thought about how much she was going to hate this project. She didn't like most of the other kids in her group. She wasn't interested in the topic. And how were they even going to begin?

Dan started to squirm. Most of the time at school, Dan felt that he didn't fit in with the rest of the kids. This was another one of those times. Norma and Debbie were real brains. They would probably think he was dumb. Chuck was kind of a wise guy, and Adam always seemed to be thinking about other worlds. And Joey — *Joey was living in another world.*

The more Debbie thought about it, the more she began to like the idea of being a ghost hunter.

"You know, this project has possibilities," she said. "But we have to have a clear hypothesis. We must do careful research. We'll perform experiments—with the proper controls, of course. *We've got to be scientific!*"

"Yeah," said Adam. "We've got to trap those ghosts!"

Chuck looked at his friend and sighed. "Look what you've gotten me into now."

Chapter Eight

IT WAS THREE O'clock. The third-graders walked in an orderly line until they reached the front door. Once they crossed the threshold, they were on their own. Some dashed off; some lingered.

Joey Baker caught up with Dan.

"He can't make me do it," said Joey. "He can't force me to be on this ghost committee. My father is a senator, and he'll stop it."

Dan didn't know what Mr. Baker did for a living, but he probably was not a senator. Dan changed the subject.

"Your brother, Matt Baker, is on my football team," said Dan.

"He's not my brother," said Joey. "We just have the same last name. I don't have any brothers or sisters."

"But I thought that Diane Baker who won the county-wide spelling bee last year was your sister."

"No," said Joey. "A lot of kids have my last name. But I'm an only child."

Norma joined Kim and Liz where they sat on a bench in the sunken garden. The sunken garden was a grassy area about the size of a large living room. It was surrounded by a brick wall with benches set against it. Three feet away from the wall, the lawn gently sloped to a smooth, flat bottom. It was a great place to sit and talk.

"Would you like to come to my house after school?" Norma asked.

"We can't," said Kim. "Liz is coming to my house today. We have to work on our committee project."

"Oh," said Norma, feeling left out. "Then I guess I'll see you tomorrow."

As she walked away, Norma did not look where she was going. She bumped into Chuck Webber, and her books went flying. Chuck helped her pick them up.

"Where are you going in such a hurry?" he asked. "Off to a big meating? Get it? A big m-e-a-t-i-n-g?"

Norma turned her back toward him and quickly walked away.

Chuck called out after her. *"Ketchup with you later, Hamburger!"*

"That guy never lets up," said Debbie, who saw the whole thing.

"I know," said Norma. "I wish I could change my name."

"Oh, don't let Chuck get to you," said Debbie. "Just give it back to him."

Norma sighed. "I never know what to say."

"That's funny," said Debbie. "You talk too little, and I talk too much."

The girls started walking.

"Hey, why don't you come to my house after school?" Debbie continued. "We can talk about our committee project. I'll show you my lab. Well, it's really just a bedroom, but I have a chemistry set and a rock collection and a battery with wires that connect to a light bulb and a piece of aluminum that shows how you need a complete circuit in order to conduct electricity."

Norma had never been to Debbie's house before. She didn't know what to expect, and she wanted some time to think about it.

"I have to stop home first and ask my mother," she said.

Chapter Nine

Norma had to walk only three short blocks to Debbie's house. She walked one block out of her way past Kim's house, but no one was outside.

When Norma found the right address, she checked it three times. She would feel very silly if she rang the wrong doorbell.

As she walked in the door, Norma was greeted by a loud bark. A big black dog jumped on her.

"Down, Buttons, down," said Debbie.

When Buttons calmed down, Norma noticed that they were standing in a small front porch with a lot of sports equipment in it. There were bicycles and skis and sneakers in every corner.

"I have three older brothers," Debbie said, as if she could read Norma's mind.

The girls walked past the dining room, where books and papers were spread out on the table. The books were fat and serious-looking. They had titles like *An Introduction to Plant Biology* and *Advanced Chemistry*.

Debbie poured two glasses of milk and put some chocolate chip cookies on a plate.

"Let's bring these to my room," Debbie said.

"Your mother lets you eat in your bedroom?" Norma asked.

"Sure," said Debbie. "Doesn't yours?"

"Only when I'm sick," Norma answered. She was very impressed.

The girls walked up the stairs and down a hall. Norma tried not to look into the bedrooms, where books and clothing were scattered on floors, desks, and unmade beds.

Though Debbie's room was small, she managed to fit lots of things in it. On her dresser were the chemistry set, the rock collection, the larger hobby battery hooked up to the light bulb, and a jar with a bone in it.

"It's a chicken bone," Debbie said. "It's in vinegar." Debbie took the bone out of the jar and bent it like a piece of rubber. "The vinegar dissolves the calcium in the bone," she explained. "Do you want to see my bread mold?"

Before Norma could answer, Debbie took something out of her closet. It was a piece of bread that had a dark layer of fuzz on it. It was not something Norma wanted to look at for long.

"Some molds are very useful," Debbie said. "They're used to make penicillin and other antibiotics that fight diseases."

Norma was glad when Debbie returned the mold to her closet.

"So how do you think we should start on our project?" Norma asked.

"Beats me," said Debbie. "I was hoping you would have some ideas."

"You know," said Norma, "I was wondering why you picked Adam to be on our committee."

Debbie blushed. "Well, I thought his belief in the supernatural would provide an interesting contrast to my own scientific approach." Then she smiled. "Besides, I think he's awfully nice."

All afternoon neither girl said another word about the ghost-hunting project. They looked at the rock collection, played with the chemistry set, and read through a book called *Magic Science Tricks.* Though no one bothered them, every few minutes Norma would hear a slamming door and heavy feet going up or down the stairs.

When it was time for Norma to go home, she was sorry to leave. On her way back, she did not even pass Kim's house. She was too busy thinking about the Clarks. She had enjoyed the messiness and disorder. It gave her an exciting feeling of freedom.

Chapter Ten

As NORMA WALKED up her driveway, she saw that her father's car was already in the garage. Dinner would be ready soon. The Hamburgers usually ate promptly at five o'clock.

"Hi, Mom! Hi, Dad! Hi, Alison!" Norma called as she walked through the kitchen door.

Everything was neat and clean as usual. Dust and mess were not allowed in the Hamburger home. Armed with mop and duster, Mrs. Hamburger was always on the lookout.

Norma headed straight for the bedroom she shared with her two-year-old sister.

"Hi, Alison," she said as she kissed the toddler on her forehead. "What bad things did you do today?" she teased.

In just a few minutes, tiny Alison could destroy things it had taken Norma her whole lifetime to collect. She tore out pictures from *Where the Wild Things Are* and scribbled on pages of *Little House on the Prairie*. She even threw Barbie down the toilet.

It was also dinnertime at the Baker house, where everyone ate in shifts. Mrs. Baker left a big pot of stew on the oven. Her twelve children would help themselves — or the older ones would help the younger ones.

Joey wasn't one of the older ones or one of the younger ones. He was somewhere in the middle. So he helped himself and sat down at the table. His brother, Matt, and his sister, Diane, were already eating.

"A guy on my football team . . . is in your class . . ." Matt said between bites. "Name is

Danny Biddicker . . . an offensive lineman . . . a good one, too. . . . You know him?"

"No," said Joey. He wasn't in the mood to talk about sports — especially sports he was bad at.

"Do you want me to help you practice your spelling words?" Diane asked.

"Sure," Joey said as he put his plate in the dishwasher. "I'm ready now."

Chapter Eleven

DAN DIDN'T HAVE to pedal so hard now that he had reached the top of the hill. His house was just at the end of the block. He decided to coast the rest of the way.

Up ahead, he heard two boys' voices. "The monster is coming! The monster is coming!"

Dan knew they were talking about him. As he rode his bicycle up the driveway, he could feel his eyes getting teary. Dan had stopped trying to make friends with those two a long time ago. But it still bothered him when they poked fun.

As Dan entered his house, a wonderful

smell led him into the kitchen. His mother was taking a batch of brownies out of the oven. She stood on tiptoes to put them high up on top of the refrigerator.

"What's that?" Dan asked.

"Incentive," said his mother. "You can have a brownie after you are weighed tomorrow. Meanwhile, have a carrot."

Football was Dan's favorite thing in the whole world. Tomorrow, he would be weighed for the Pop Warner team. Since he was already too big to play with the other third-graders, he would be playing with the fourth-graders this year. That was fine with him. But if he gained any more weight, he would have to play with the fifth grade. Those boys were much older, smarter, and tougher. Dan was afraid of them.

As soon as he started his spelling homework, Dan's mind began to wander. He thought about the strange project, and he wondered why Chuck had picked him to be on the committee. Maybe Chuck wasn't such a bad guy after all.

Chapter Twelve

FOR THE NEXT two weeks, Mr. Jenkins's class would break up into committees at two o'clock every afternoon. After two weeks, each committee would give a report.

At the first meeting, the psychic investigation committee discovered it had lost one of its members. Joey Baker brought a note from home. He could not be in the ghost-hunting group because of "personal reasons."

"I should have thought of that," Chuck said.

The others ignored him.

"So how do we begin?" Debbie asked.

No one had an answer.

The rest of the class was humming with busy voices. The ghost hunters were perfectly silent until Adam asked, "Why are skeletons empty-headed?"

The others said nothing. They were all feeling pretty empty-headed themselves. And not in the mood for a joke.

"Because they have nothing between their ears!" Adam said.

No one laughed. They were too busy thinking about how much fun they would have on other committees.

"Cheer up, guys," Adam said. "Let's make the best of it. There could be a real ghost here! We could be famous!"

"Or we could be dead," said Chuck.

"Or we could fail," said Norma.

"Or we could discover the truth," said Debbie.

"Well, what do you think?" Chuck asked Dan.

Dan had something to say, but he was too shy. What if it made him sound dumb?

"I think . . . I think . . . we're not going to get anywhere like this," said Dan. "Like it or not, we're a team. And in a team everyone has to do his or her part. And . . . and . . . and . . . it doesn't matter whether you win or lose. It's how you play the game." Dan was so embarrassed. He could feel his face get pink . . . then red . . . then maroon.

"Dan's right," Norma said. "Mr. Jenkins won't care whether we find ghosts or not. What really matters is how hard we try."

For the first time ever, Dan didn't feel quite so dumb.

"I'll go to the library and see if there are any old newspaper stories about Blackwell House," said Norma.

"As I've been saying all along," Debbie added, "I believe there's a reasonable explanation. My uncle is an electrician. Maybe he can find something wrong with the wires."

"My dad is a plumber. Maybe he can find something," Dan offered.

"I still think it's a ghost," said Adam. "A restless spirit who is having some fun scaring third-graders.

"Chuck, do you remember that stone in the bushes? I'll see if I can find out anything about that boy."

"I'll interview the kids at school," said Chuck. "I'll ask them if they've noticed anything weird lately."

"You should talk to the teachers and the other grown-ups who work here, too," Norma suggested.

"Thanks," said Chuck. "Brains like yours are rare — medium rare."

"Cut it out," said Norma.

Chuck laughed. "Have it *your* way!"

Chapter Thirteen

ON THURSDAY, DEBBIE'S uncle checked the electricity. Debbie took notes as he looked at wires, fuses, and outlets.

"Everything is in order," he said.

On Friday, Dan's father checked the plumbing.

"Your ghost isn't here," said Mr. Biddicker.

On Saturday, Adam went to the library. He looked in the card catalog, but he found nothing under Thomas Jackson Blackwell. Then he looked under ghosts. Adam was in luck. There were three books about ghosts, and they were all on the shelves.

Adam started to read one of them. It had stories about lots of ghosts — young ghosts, old ghosts, friendly ghosts, and nasty ghosts. All the ghosts had one thing in common. As people, they had died tragically.

"That must be it," said Adam. "Thomas Jackson Blackwell must have had a tragic death. He's mad about something. And that's why he's haunting Blackwell House!"

Adam had to find out more. He went to the librarian.

"We don't have anything here about Thomas Jackson Blackwell," said Mrs. Weitz. "But why don't you try the Historical Society. Just ask for Mr. Barry."

The Elmwood Historical Society was near the river on North Main Street. The building was very old and unfriendly. Adam waited a few minutes before he opened the door.

The first thing he saw when he walked inside was a sign: FREDERICK DAVID BLACKWELL: THE EARLY YEARS.

It was an art show. Along each wall was a row of paintings. Adam looked at the paintings, but he did not know what he was supposed to be seeing.

One painting looked like the scribbles of his younger brother: a big yellow face with two dot eyes and a blue and pink smudged mouth. Another one looked like a big yellow pickle sitting on two leaves against a black background.

"Can I help you, young man?" asked the guard.

"Mr. Barry?" Adam asked shyly.

The guard pointed toward an open door down the hall.

When Adam reached the office, Mr. Barry was busy talking to a very old man with a long beard and thick glasses. As Adam waited, he heard words he could not understand.

"... concentric bands of diminishing color intensity ..." mumble, mumble, "... plastic objects and sensations from within and without ..." mumble, mumble.

Finally, the younger man looked up.

"What can I do for you?" he asked.

"I'm trying to find out about Thomas Jackson Blackwell," Adam said.

"Well, maybe I can help you," said the old man. "I'm Frederick David Blackwell. Thomas was Grandfather's younger brother."

Adam had never met a real artist before. He didn't know what to say. He might say he liked the paintings. But he wasn't sure if he did.

Adam tried to play it safe. "It must have taken a long time for you to paint all these pictures."

Mr. Blackwell smiled kindly. "The pictures in this exhibition were painted over a ten-year period when I was experimenting with abstract expressionism. Let me show you my favorite."

Mr. Blackwell led Adam to a painting with three circles. The circles were very dark in the middle and lighter toward the outside.

"Foghorns," said Mr. Blackwell.

All of a sudden, Adam could see the foghorns. He could hear them, too, with their loud honking noise, so strong in the center and getting softer as it spread.

"Now what did you want to know about Thomas?" Mr. Blackwell asked.

Adam didn't know what to say. Would Mr. Blackwell get angry when he asked about Thomas's ghost? Would he laugh? Finally, Adam began by telling Mr. Blackwell all about his committee project. Then he got up enough courage to ask him about Thomas Jackson Blackwell.

The old man stroked his beard. "Well," he said, "I believe Thomas did die tragically. It was during the Civil War. Soldiers were gathering for a battle. Thomas went to warn the neighbors, but he did not reach safety before the battle began.

"Does this help your investigation, Adam?"

"It helps a lot. Thanks," said Adam. "You know, most people say I'm silly to think about ghosts. They say I have a wild imagination."

Mr. Blackwell laughed. "Well, I think a wild imagination is a good thing to have. So, tell me, Adam, are you an art lover?"

"I am now," Adam said.

Adam was convinced. They were dealing

with a real ghost. On Monday, he told the story to the rest of his committee.

"It all fits," said Adam.

"No, it doesn't," said Norma. "He doesn't sound like the kind of kid who would go around pushing pencils off desks and flickering lights and scaring third-graders."

"Well, maybe he just got tired of being such a goody-goody all the time," said Chuck. "Maybe he wanted to cut loose for a change."

Norma thought about it for a minute.

"You may be right," she said. "Or maybe he just wanted some attention."

Chapter Fourteen

IT WAS CHUCK'S turn to tell the others what he'd found out. For three days, he interviewed classmates, teachers, and even Mr. Johnson, the caretaker. He carried his tape recorder and microphone everywhere. But he wasn't at all happy with his results.

"Here goes nothing," Chuck said as he turned on the tape recorder.

For a few seconds, all they heard was static. Then. . .

Chuck: Testing . . . testing . . . one, two, three . . . testing.

In the background: Policeman, policeman,
Do your duty.
Here comes Lori
The American beauty.

Chuck: I will now be talking to Jenny Carle from Class 3-B. ... Miss Carle, I am investigating reports of psychic disturbances at Blackwell House. Could you tell me if you have noticed anything unusual?

Jenny Carle: Get lost, Chuck.

Chuck: Hey, this is part of my report. You've gotta help me.

In the background: Salute to the captain,
Curtsy to the queen

Jenny: So, what do you want to know?

Chuck: I want to know if you've seen anything strange lately — besides the sight of your own face in the mirror.

Jenny: I repeat — GET LOST!

(Pause)

Chuck: I will now be talking to Lori Marino from Class 3-B. ... I am investigating reports of psychic disturbances at Blackwell House,

Miss Marino. Have you noticed anything unusual?

Lori: Well, there was the time when all the pencils fell off the desks and the globe fell off the shelf and the lights flickered.

Chuck: Anything else?

Lori: Isn't that enough?

Chuck: Thanks, Lori. . . . I will now be talking to Joey Baker from Class 3-B and Steve Wells from Class 3-A. . . . Have you noticed anything spooky lately?

Joey: I sure did! It was in the boys' room! A ghost! I saw him with my own eyes! No fooling! Honest! I swear!

Chuck: What about you, Steve?

Steve: Nah, I don't believe in that stuff. Nothing ever happened in our classroom.

A voice: Nothing ever happened in our classroom, either. You guys in 3-B are just a bunch of scaredy-cats.

Chuck: That was Jeff Arnold from Class 3-C. And I'm gonna make him take that back.

(Pause)

Chuck: Mr. Jenkins, I'm investigating reports

of psychic disturbances at Blackwell House. Have you noticed anything unusual?

Mr. Jenkins: Good work, Chuck. ... Uh, no comment.

(Pause)

Chuck: I am now talking to Mr. Johnson, the caretaker of Blackwell House. Mr. Johnson lives over in the carriage house just about forty yards away. Mr. Johnson, I am investigating reports of psychic disturbances at Blackwell House. Have you noticed anything unusual lately?

Mr. Johnson: Why, now that you mention it, Chuckie Boy, I believe I did. Last night, I was watching *The Late, Late Movie* when I fell asleep in front of the set. By the time I woke up, the station had gone off the air. There was nothing but that fuzzy stuff on the tube.

All of a sudden, a face appeared on the screen. It had no hair ... no teeth ... no eyes. But it had a mouth — and it spoke.

"Help, help me, Mr. Johnson," it said. "I'm trapped in your television set."

It was the most horrible thing I had ever

seen. But even so, I couldn't turn down a plea for help. I had to think fast. Then I realized there was only one thing to do.

Chuck: What was that?

Mr. Johnson: To turn off the TV. I turned it off and went to bed.

Chuck: Uh, Mr. Johnson, you aren't pulling my leg, are you?

Mr. Johnson: Why would I do that?

Chuck: Are you sure you aren't getting back at me for the time I bent your car antenna with a soccer ball?

Mr. Johnson: Nah.

Chuck: Or for the time I hit the baseball through your bathroom window when you were taking a shower?

Mr. Johnson: You sure took me by surprise.

Chuck: Well, er, thank you, Mr. Johnson.

Chapter Fifteen

"I'M AFRAID I CAN'T believe some of your witnesses," said Debbie.

"What a bummer!" said Chuck. "Not one good clue after all my work."

Adam wanted to make him feel better. "That's the way it goes sometimes."

"Well, you're not going to believe what I have, either," said Norma, "although these are from a pretty good source. They're newspaper articles — one from ten years ago, the other from eighteen years ago."

"Where did you get them?" Danny asked.

"At the library," Norma answered. "Every year, all the articles in the newspaper are listed in a big book. You just tell the librarian the date of the paper you want, and she'll get it for you. Sometimes it's just a regular newspaper, and sometimes it's on film. You can make copies, too. See for yourselves."

The committee passed around the stories. They were hard to read because the type was so small. But they were worth the struggle.

Mysterious Force Haunts Elmwood Family

ELMWOOD, October 8 — A mysterious force has caused strange disturbances at the home of Elias T. Blackwell. For the last three days, objects have fallen from walls and jumped from tables. A lamp danced across a desk and crashed on the floor while a vase filled with flowers toppled over.

The Bacon County police continue their search for the cause of these mysterious disturbances.

This was followed by other articles: "Police Baffled by Elmond Mystery," "Joint Still Jumpin' in Elmwood"— and finally "Family Flees Mystery House."

Elias T. Blackwell and his family gave in to the ghosts and moved away. The next article appeared eight years later. By then, Blackwell House had been empty for a long time.

Students Report New Blackwell House Haunting

ELMWOOD, July 11 — Two students reported strange disturbances in Blackwell House while seeking shelter from last night's storm. The students, James F. Riley and John W. Jenkins, both from Plumtree County, described unusual screeches and knocks, followed by a loud explosion. The students had previously searched the abandoned house and found it to be empty. Police are baffled by this report, which recalls other mysterious activities that occurred in the house eight years ago.

Adam was surprised. Lisa's story about the two students was true!

"Do you think that John W. Jenkins is *our* Mr. Jenkins?" Adam asked.

"Could be," said Chuck.

"I wonder what that means," said Norma.

"Well, if we really want to find out what's

going on, there's only one thing to do," said Adam.

"I don't want to hear this," said Chuck.

"One of us should see what goes on here in the dark," Adam continued. "Someone should come here at night."

"We'll never get permission," said Norma.

"Then we'll have to do it *without* permission," said Adam. "Any volunteers?"

Everyone was quiet. Then Chuck broke the silence. "Since Debbie doesn't believe in ghosts, I think she should go."

"Thanks, Chuck," said Debbie. "But I do believe in murderers. Why don't you go? Your big mouth could scare off anything."

"Time out," said Dan. "Remember, we're all in this together. I say we should all go."

"Count me out," said Chuck. "I've got to stay home that night and take a bath."

Norma had never done anything this bad before. "I'll go," she said. Good-bye, goody-goody.

"Me, too," said Debbie.

"I'll go," said Adam and Dan.

"Oh, all right. I'll go, too," said Chuck.

"Then it's settled," said Adam. "We'll meet at the corner of Blackwell Road at nine o'clock. Everyone bring a flashlight."

After school, Adam went straight home. He couldn't believe he was going on a real ghost hunt! This was the most exciting thing that had ever happened to him!

Adam spent all afternoon reading one of the library books he had checked out on Saturday. It was called *The World's Most Famous Ghosts*. By nighttime, Adam knew about every ghost that anyone had ever claimed to see. And he was scared stiff.

At eight-thirty, Adam pretended to go to bed. Fifteen minutes later, he climbed out of his bedroom window. He was on his way to a big adventure.

Adam was the first to reach Blackwell Road. The moon wore a sinister face that night. It cast an eerie glow. Adam looked down the road. Was he looking at two rows of trees or the hands and arms of a dozen witches? He shivered.

"I ain't 'fraid of no ghosts," Adam tried to remind himself.

A hand grabbed his shoulder.

I'm dead! he thought.

Chapter Sixteen

"ADAM, IT'S ME," said Joey Baker.

"What are you doing here?" Adam asked.

"I couldn't be on the river committee because I get seasick. So I came back to be with you guys. I called Debbie, and she told me to meet everyone here."

Meanwhile, Chuck caught up with Norma on the way. "How ya doing, Hamburger? Where's the beef?"

Norma decided she had had enough. "Why do you do it?" she asked. "Why are you always making fun of me?"

Chuck was surprised. "I don't know," he said. "I just like to make jokes. I don't mean anything bad by it. I'm sorry."

"Oh, forget it," Norma said. "I'm beginning to get used to it."

By nine o'clock, everyone but Dan had gathered at Blackwell Road. Ten minutes later, a shadowy figure could be seen running toward them.

"Wait up!" he shouted. "My mother couldn't believe I wanted to go to bed so early," said Dan. "She thought I had to be sick. She kept taking my temperature and feeling my forehead. I thought I'd never get away."

In the moonlight, Blackwell Road looked creepier than ever. To keep up their courage, the third-graders traded monster riddles.

"What animal can't be found in a haunted house?" Chuck asked.

"A scaredy-cat!" said Norma.

Chuck was annoyed. "Lucky guess, Hamburger," he said.

Adam had a riddle, too. "What keeps flies out of a haunted house?"

No one could get that one.

"Window screams!" Adam shouted.

When they finally saw the building, Joey wanted to turn back. The others did not want to admit it, but they were afraid, too.

Blackwell House looked more haunted than ever. Its windows seemed to glare with anger. Its towers looked as if they held evil secrets.

"Let's stick together," Adam said as they walked around the house.

Then they found what they were looking for. An open window. Dan tried to open it wide enough for everyone to fit, but it was stuck. Only Joey Baker was small enough to go through.

"Just climb in and open the side door," said Adam.

"Not a chance," said Joey. "What happened to 'Let's stick together'?"

"Look, Joey, this is our only chance. You've got to do it," said Debbie.

"Yeah, Joey. Come on, Joey," said the others.

Joey had never been so important before. It felt good.

"Okay," he said. And with a boost from Dan, Joey shimmied through the window. He ran to the door and let the others in.

The third-graders found themselves in the kitchen. They were fascinated. None of them had ever been in the kitchen before.

Giant pots were stacked on the stove and refrigerator. Chuck couldn't resist. He opened the refrigerator door.

"Looks like we're having hot dogs tomorrow," he said.

"Can't we turn on some lights?" Debbie asked.

"Bad idea," said Adam. "Mr. Johnson might see them and find us here."

"Let's look around," said Dan.

They followed their flashlights through the cafeteria and into the large assembly room. They looked inside the three downstairs offices. Everything seemed to be all right.

Then they heard a sound. It was like the

tinkling of glass. And it was coming from the teachers' lounge.

Chuck opened the door.

"A ghost!" he shouted.

Joey screamed.

"It's just a curtain," said Adam. "And the noise was just the light fixture. Let's go upstairs."

The boys' room and the girls' room were on the second floor.

"We'll have to split up," said Adam.

"Hey, that's not fair," said Debbie. "There are four of you and only two of us."

"We'll be all right," said Norma.

Hand in hand, the girls walked in.

"You know," said Debbie, "you're the best friend I've ever had."

Norma gave Debbie's hand a squeeze. "And you're the best friend I've ever had. Now, let's get out of here while we're still alive."

"Nothing in there," said Adam. "Let's look in the classrooms."

There was nothing unusual about Ms. Carpenter's classroom or Mrs. Goodman's classroom.

Next was Miss Brady's room. It was directly below Mr. Jenkins's.

"The door is stuck," Adam said.

"I'll do it," said Dan.

One big push and it was open.

"I don't like this room," said Joey. "It has cracks all over the walls."

"Hey, look," said Debbie. "Tomorrow's spelling lesson is on the board. We already had those words a month ago!"

All of a sudden, they heard footsteps from above. They were slow and heavy.

THUMP. THUMP. THUMP. THUMP.

"Listen," said Adam.

The footsteps seemed to change. They became quick and light.

Pitter-patter-pitter-patter-pitter-patter.

"I'm scared," said Joey.

"Someone or something is in our classroom," said Norma. The doors began to rattle.

"Let's get out of here!" said Chuck. The walls shook. The ghost hunters dashed down the stairs.

Then CLUNK! went the pots in the kitchen and CRASH! went the light fixture in the lounge.

"I'm going upstairs to see what this is all about," said Adam.

He ran up to the third floor with Dan, Debbie, Norma, and Chuck running close behind.

"Wait for me," Joey cried. He did not want to be left alone.

Standing outside their own classroom, the third-graders heard a knock on the wall. The door shook. Adam's hand trembled as he touched the knob. The knocking continued. Adam pushed the door open.

All eyes went to the board where an eerie, glowing face grinned back at them. Adam felt his hair stand on end. Joey screamed. Norma covered her mouth, Debbie her eyes. Dan threw an eraser at it.

Norma turned on the light—and the face disappeared. Then Adam had an idea. He turned off the light, and the face reappeared. He turned on the light, and it went away again. Light off, it appeared. Light on, it disappeared.

The others began to catch on, too. "That isn't a ghost," said Adam. "It's just plain old moonlight coming in from that weird window."

Meanwhile, the banging and knocking grew louder.

"I want to call for a vote," said Norma. "All those in favor of keeping the lights on, say 'Aye.'"

"Aye," said Chuck.

"Aye," said Joey.

"Aye," said Debbie and Dan.

"Aye," said Adam.

Then the door slammed shut.

Once again, Adam had a hard time opening a door.

"Sure glad you're around," he said to Dan.

Dan put his foot on the wall for leverage and pulled with all his strength. The others cheered as the door flew open.

"There sure is something wrong with the

doors in this place," said Debbie. "This could be a clue."

As they continued their search, the ghost hunters noticed that about half of the doors didn't fit their frames. And a few of the walls had bad cracks.

The third-graders were gathered in the ground floor hallway. Everything had been quiet for a while.

Suddenly, the house began to rattle and shake.

"It feels like we're sinking," said Norma.

"It sure does," said Adam. "Let's get out of here."

The third-graders ran out the door and into the garden.

Chapter Seventeen

"YOU KNOW," SAID Adam, "this reminds me of a movie I saw. A family moved into a new house that turned out to be haunted. Their little girl was taken into the spirit world. The only way they could talk to her was through the TV set.

"It turned out that the house had been built over a cemetery. The spirits were angry. Skeletons came out of the ground and tried to force the family to move away, which they did, of course."

"Somehow, I don't think that's the case here," said Norma.

"But maybe we should look around. We might find some more clues," said Debbie.

The third-graders split up and began the search. Suddenly, Joey shouted. "Help! Help!"

The others ran to him. Joey was stuck. He was up to his waist in a hole.

"I just stepped into these bushes and fell through," he said.

Dan grabbed him under the arms and pulled him out. Adam bent over the edge of the hole and looked inside with his flashlight.

"There's a tunnel down there. Let's see where it goes," he suggested.

"No way," Joey whined. "I'm staying out here."

"Then you'll be staying out here alone," said Debbie.

Joey sighed. "Oh, all right."

One by one, the third-graders climbed into the tunnel. The shorter kids could stand up straight. But Chuck, Dan, and Debbie had to bend over.

As they entered, their feet sank in the soft mud. They tried not to touch the stone walls, which were covered with slime and mold. It was very dark and creepy. The children walked slowly in single file. Joey pushed ahead of Debbie. "I don't want to be last," he said.

Everyone was quiet. The children were alert to every sight and sound.

Squish, squish, squish. Squish, squish, squish.

"What's that noise?" Adam asked.

"I think it's our shoes," said Norma.

Squish, squish, squish.

Crackle, crackle, crackle.

"Now what's that noise," Norma asked.

"What noise?" said Debbie.

Crackle, crackle, crackle.

"That noise," said Norma.

"It's just my candy bar wrapper," said Chuck. "You want some?"

"You know," said Adam. "This reminds me of a movie where a bunch of giant ants — and I mean GIANT ants — the size of a big truck — kidnap two boys and take them into the sewers of Los Angeles."

"You watch too many movies, Adam," said Norma.

"No," said Debbie. "Adam could be onto something. This could be an old storm sewer. I'll bet it leads right to the river. Let's keep going."

The children walked along in the darkness. Their flashlights helped them see the muddy ground. But up ahead was the black unknown.

"Hey, Dan, do you think there are any mice in here?" Joey asked.

"Possibly," said Dan.

"Hey, Dan, do you think there are any snakes in here?" Joey asked.

"Probably." Dan felt his hair go stiff. He was afraid of snakes and mice, too.

"Maybe someone lives here," said Joey. "Maybe some mean, horrible murderer who hates children!"

"CUT IT OUT!" Chuck shouted. "You're making it worse."

The children imagined they felt worms in their hair and mice at their feet.

Dan was too frightened to take another step. Then he had an idea.

"Anybody have any more jokes?" he asked.

"I have one," said Chuck. "There was an *old* lady who lived *all* alone. One day, she hears the telephone ring. When she picks up the phone, she hears a low, mysterious voice that says, '*I am the viper!*' "

"Is this what you call a joke?" Debbie interrupted.

"Cut it out," said Chuck. "You're ruining my delivery.

"She hangs up. Five minutes later, the

phone rings again. She picks it up and hears the same low, mysterious voice. *'I am the viper!'* She hangs up. Five minutes later, the doorbell rings. She listens through the intercom and hears, *'I am the viper!'*

"She doesn't know what to do. She can't stand the suspense.

"Then she sees a little old man with a bucket and mop. *'I am the viper,'* he says, *'I've come to vash and vipe the vindows.'* "

Everyone was laughing. Then Dan stopped.

"We've reached the end," he said. "The rest is blocked up."

"Look!" Norma whispered.

Everyone turned around. A white light shone brightly from where they'd entered.

"Who's there?" a voice called.

"It's the murderer who hates children!" Joey screamed.

"Calm down. It sounds like Mr. Johnson," said Chuck. "It's Chuck Webber, Mr. Johnson. I'm here with some other kids."

"What are you kids doing?" the caretaker asked.

"Er, we're investigating reports of psychic disturbances," said Chuck.

"Ah, yes," said Mr. Johnson. "Well, you'd better take your psychic investigation somewhere else. This sewer can get mighty full when the river is high.

"Get in my truck," he said once they had all crawled out of the tunnel. "I'll take you kids home."

Chapter Eighteen

PAUL LUCAS WAS droning on and on. The transportation committee was giving its report.

Adam struggled to stay awake. He hadn't gotten to sleep until midnight. Then Paul said something interesting about the river. The river was tidal. That meant the water level went up and down. Suddenly Adam remembered. Mr. Johnson had said that the sewer got full when the river was high.

Adam passed a note to the rest of the kids on his committee:

MEET AFTER SCHOOL AT THE SUNKEN

GARDEN

At three o'clock, they were all together.

"I think we're onto something," said Adam. "Paul Lucas said that the water level in the river goes up and down."

"And Mr. Johnson said the sewer gets fuller when the river is high," Joey added.

"Right," said Debbie. "The floodwater seeps through and floods the sewer, and the soil becomes waterlogged."

"And the building shifts," Norma said.

Dan was excited. Being smart was getting easier all the time. *"Blackwell House is sinking!"*

"And that," Chuck added, "is where all the bangs and slams and rattles come from."

"That's too bad," said Adam. "I was really hoping we'd find a ghost."

Adam decided to rethink his future. Instead of being a ghost hunter like the *Ghostbusters,* he could become an artist like Mr. Blackwell.

The next day, the ghost hunters gave their report. Mr. Jenkins was very impressed. He had been curious about Blackwell House ever since he had stayed there as a student.

Suddenly, he became very serious. "This could be dangerous," he said. "I'd better report this right away."

Building inspectors arrived that afternoon and closed the school. Everyone was sent home early. For the next two weeks, the whole third grade relocated to a church basement. Meanwhile, the sewer was filled, and Blackwell House was repaired.

Now the third grade was safe, thanks to the ghost committee. Mr. Jenkins gave them all A's, and the mayor gave them a special citation.

The communication committee had a

great story to write about. On the front page of the *Elmwood Independent* was a big picture of Adam, Norma, Dan, Debbie, Joey, and Chuck with their arms around one another. And above the picture was a big headline:

WE AIN'T 'FRAID OF NO GHOSTS!